It was simple, until it wasn't

Chelsea-Victoria

DEDICATION

To those who feel unlovable; you are valued and appreciated. You are unique and special and there is always someone out there who will love and appreciate you for exactly who you are. Keep shining, and never let anyone dull your sparkle.

Table of Contents

ACKNOWLEDGMENTS

Special thanks to Jesus, for waking me up every morning to write this love story.

Thank you to every romance author that I read, for giving me the inspiration I

needed, to put my stories on paper.

Chapter 1: Stuck

It was simple, until it wasn't.

As I stand here, at the door of the Eugene Lang College of Liberal Arts, my mind just races. I'm thinking so many thoughts, seeing so many things, hearing so many sounds, I can see a future here. Or do I. All I have ever wanted is to step somewhere where I feel accepted. To step into a circle where I can really say "I'm Home" (that isn't my room of course.) As I stare at that water-clear glass door, I can't help but think of all the memories, of all the days I've waited for this. I've also said that this was my dream, but now that it's here; I'm feeling shaky. I know, I know, no time to feel shaky when your destiny awaits you. It's like my whole life I've been pushing on the door that I'm staring into, but now that I'm finally here, I don't know how I feel. Of course I want this, but I can't help but think...what if there's more?

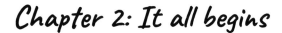

Chapter 2: It all begins

It was simple, until it wasn't.

On March 7th, I was born. My parents named me Kemina Marcheline. When you translate both of my names you literally get "strong warrior." I'm not sure what my parents were thinking when they named me; I'm the opposite of strong. Anyways, I wasn't really the... "typical" kid. Most kids ran around naked, or played outside all the time. Not me. I just kinda sat there. My Mother tells me that I was always deep in thought, even as a little child. I wasn't adventurous, but I was always thinking. By the time I was 4 years old, I could read fluently. And I don't mean those small picture books, no. I mean actual novels, Like Wonder, or those Reader's digest books. By the time I was 6 I had read every one that we had in the house. Then I moved on to Nancy Drew, Then the Hardy Boys. I was like those caterpillars who munch through a ton of leaves and then their bodies get huge; except the leaves were my books, and the body was my mind. Reading gave me my imagination, and all of this random information that 9 times out of 10, you will never need in your life, became my safe-haven. My first love was my books. Well, when you turn 6 years old, school now comes into play. Wilemina's school for the children of the world. Dramatic much? Well I started there and didn't leave until I graduated high school.

The downfall of Wilemina's school was that because you were there from the time that you're 6 to the time that you're 18, is that you get judged from day one and usually, that determines the rest of your time. Well, as a 6 year old girl, I didn't talk much. I would have much rather been in a book or day-dreaming off in a corner. This got me labeled as a weird kid, a threat. I didn't really have any friends. That was fine with me, but to everyone else it was just fuel to make fun of me. Kids are cruel. Long story short, Wilhemina's was hell. But you know what was heaven for me? My books. Teachers loved having me in their classes, I didn't talk but I always listened; and my grades were impeccable. They never wavered. I kept my grades high because they were something that no one could take away from me. The only thing that only I had. So of course, just like in every high school; I became the nerdy girl whose head is always stuck in a book, and that was that.

Let's see, I covered my extensive love for books, and my love for learning and keeping my grades high...what am I forgetting? Ha, how could I forget? The whole reason you're probably still even reading is to figure out why I was at some door and why I couldn't go in.

When I gave the whole run-down, I failed to mention that I was also a music kid. I excelled in it. My music teacher somehow recognized that I had a knack for it when I was 6 years old. I play piano and guitar, and that's what also helped me get through school at Wilhemina's.

I got my first camera when I was in 5th grade. We were going on a class field trip to the zoo, so I got one of those disposable ones. When I showed my parents the pictures I had taken, they just stood there staring in shock. That Christmas I was given a Nikon D-3500 camera from my father. I had no idea that the camera would take me to such amazing places. I started off by taking pictures of small things, like bees, or flowers. Soon I started doing bigger things like people. My favorite part about my photography was capturing the imperfect. I feel like the world is so obsessed with this impossible "perfect" so I take pictures of the imperfect. If you look through my SD card on my camera, you'll find silly ones, beautiful ones, ugly ones; My favorite photos are ones that have a beautiful subject, but have something else happening in the background of them. It just...works. Pictures where my subject is laughing are also ones that I love. When I take pictures, I attempt to capture humanity, and I succeed. I entered my first photography contest when I was 13 and won it. The judges' note stated "you do a remarkable thing, Kemina; You capture the real in a world where the fake is the real." That comment sticks with me today, and fuels me.

Now that I've actually given you the full and complete rundown, I think you are ready. Ready to know what got me to that door.

It all started with an assembly. Everyone at Wilhelmina's knows that when they call assembly's, it's either really important, or really not. This assembly in particular was only for the seniors. So we file into the gym, and our principal, Mrs. Wake list taps on the microphone, testing it.

"Good morning students"

Groggily we replied back "Good morning"

Mrs. Wake-list goes on and talks about a few announcements and upcoming events at the school, but then she gets to the meat of the assembly. College. Now, I have done some research on college, but not nearly enough. She explained that it was now college application season, and that we needed to work on our applications and send them to our choices swiftly. I knew what I wanted to do; photograph musicians and artists, and work with film; but I had no idea where I even wanted to go. Although I said that I wasn't an ambitious girl, I did want to go everywhere, and see all there was to be seen. I wanted just my camera and some music to tour the world. I realized that I needed to find perhaps an exchange program (for traveling) or a photography program, or even a piano performance program. And the journey began. This should be easy right?

Wrong.

Looking for colleges that interested me was like looking for needles in my big afro. You know they are there but you simply cannot find them. I decided to settle on 3 schools, The Eugene Lang College of liberal arts, The University of Southern California, and The School of Cinematic Arts. It took quite a bit of time, but I finished my applications for all 3 schools, and began wishing on every star and quazart around that I would be accepted to one of them. Of course, the submitting of the application wasn't the hard part of the process, it was the waiting for results and responses that was.

You want to know why I couldn't walk through that door?

Ps. It's everything that happened during this waiting period

At this point, it's February. Things are still normal, Wilhemina's is still Wilhemina's, hella dramatic; the kids are still mean, and it still weirdly smells like chlorine everywhere you go in that building. My photography is going great, and I had just booked a photoshoot with one of my mother's friends. This is a little important, because If I do well with this shoot, it may put me on the map. If I can be put on the map for photography, it could change my whole life.

Anyways, I was eating my lunch in the hallway, pretty typical of the high-school-nerd. I was always alone at Wilhemina's. That is, until that random day in February. Figures, it happened to be the 29th because we finally had a leap year. Something weird is bound to happen on leap year days...

I keep getting carried away. Just as I was then. Sitting, lost in thought about God knows what. It could have been anything from my father, to Electron configuration. I was pulled out of my thoughts by this guy sitting down next to me. Of course, I was confused as to all-get out. I'm the school nerd, absolutely no-one wants to interact with me, and they haven't since I even began school here. With all of that being said, who in the world is this, and why in the world would they sit next to me.

He was new. When you have gone to school with the same kids that you've been with since you were 6 years old, you know everyone in and out. This kid? Never seen him once. He just sat down, and didn't say much for a second. I am so awkward, and my heart was racing; but I somehow mustered up the courage to say:

"Hi"

He smiled a little

"Hi"

"Are you new?"

"Yes. It's my second day"

"Oh..."

He nodded his head a little "Oh is right, it's day 2 and I already don't feel like I should be here."

I chuckled a little bit. "Yeah... if you can't tell, I don't feel like I should be here either, honestly never have"

He chuckled a little. "I'm Matthew, but my friends know me as Mark."

I looked at him, a little confused "How did they manage to get Mark from Matthew?"

He laughed outwardly this time "Funny. First it came from the sequence of bible chapters; Matthew, Mark, Luke and John. Secondly I love art. I seriously love art. I'm always marking something."

This made me smile. Art wasn't something that the kids at Wilhelmina were into, it was known as "nerd crap" for old people.

Listen, I'm not that kind of girl but as I kept looking at him and talking to him, I found him very pretty. He had the most beautiful caramel skin, and pretty hair that he kept in a man-bun. I'll never admit it out loud but I am a sucker for long hair. Not long-unkempt hair like Jay-Z; but long, well-taken care of hair like Brandon Lake. Matthew's hair was long, but it was obvious that he took care of it. He was definitely going to get crap for that at this school, these kids are still holding on to 1930's long hair for girls ideas.

I separated my brain from admiring him so that I could continue the conversation.

"My name is Kemina-Marcheline, but my friends know me as Mina." I don't know why I said that.The only person that ever called me Mina was my friend Denise, and she's been dead a year.

He was looking at me directly in my eyes. "Kemina-Marcheline..." He paused for a moment, looked me up and down, then returned to my eyes.

"I think that is the most beautiful name that I have ever heard in my life"

He began to chuckle.

I chuckled too "What?"

Then he asked me something that I never saw coming.

"Kemina-Marcheline, would you do me the absolute honors of allowing me to draw you?"

My goodness is it hard to tell him no.

Chapter 3: Yes

I nodded my head, and he smiled. If I were any lighter than I was, you would have been able to see my whole face turn tomato-red.

I figured that since he was new, he was going to make friends, and forget about me rather quickly, so I decided to force myself not to put any mind to him. But every single day he came to sit with me in that hallway. It was now April and I was waiting for college decisions.

"Kemina-Marcheline, scootch." He commanded. I grabbed my jacket and camera bag and placed it on the other side of me. I loved how he called me my full name. Something about it made me feel happy, and seen. He looked at me in my eyes and then began to frown.

"Kemina-Marcheline? Are you okay? Why do you look so flushed?"

I forget that he's an artist sometimes. He can detect small color changes that most of the kids at Wilhelmina couldn't. I had been crying for all of my first 3 periods that day, and I was trying to console myself right before Mark got there.

"Yeah, I'm okay."

Mark gave me the sternest look with the most serious face that I had ever seen his goofy self give.

"Kemina-Marcheline, I know that I haven't known you your entire life, and I know that we only spend lunch together, but I know you.

13

Kemina-Marcheline, I know you. And I don't think you're okay."

That's when it hit me. Mark was right. I knew him better than I knew anyone else, and he knew me better than I gave him credit for.

"Mark, I trust you."

He smiled at me. "Kemina-Marcheline, I trust you. If you want to talk to me then I'll listen. If you want me to sit here and shut-up then I'll sit here and shut-up. I just want you to know that I care."

I had never had the courage to tell anyone about Denise, but with Mark it was different. He made me feel safe. He made me feel safe to exist, safe to love, safe to be myself. So I allowed myself to open up.

"It's... It's April 21st. Last year, today the only friend I had died. Her name was Denise. She loved children, and volleyball. She loved me. We would do just about everything together. We didn't go to the same school, but we were essentially sisters." I smiled a little bit, thinking of her always doing that. But where the smiles came from, so did the tears. " Denise used to write the most beautiful poetry. She would write a lot of her poems for me. I have never forgiven myself for not telling her to publish them while she was still alive, while she could." My hands started to shake and my nose turned red, like it always does when I cry. "She was incredible. She was diagnosed with brest cancer when she was 13= and she continued to fight it

14

until she turned 18 last year. She was doing so well- they even said she could

come off of Chemo. It was so simple until it wasn't."

"I came home from school last year to my parents in the kitchen. and they

told me she was gone. She lost her battle to cancer, and I'm still here."

I couldn't bear it anymore, and the waterworks fell. They didn't stop either.

Most of them were silent, but I could feel every bit of her spirit around me.

Mark had tears in his eyes too. He grabbed me and pulled me into an

embrace. I was so thankful for him at that moment, as he just let me cry

into his chest. He just held me, as I became almost unconsolable and kept

telling me how proud he was of me. The rest of that day was difficult. I

didn't pay attention at all in class, and I failed my chemistry quiz because I

quite literally couldn't pay attention.

When I came home, I was tired. Mama had made dinner. She must've

known what day it was because she made my favorite, Turkey-Strovenaugh

and a cupcake with a blue butterfly on it. There was a note too.

"I love you, baby. I have to work another shift this evening, but soon we will

go out and shop, get our nails done, whatever you want to do."

That's one thing about my mama, she might work a whole lot, but when we

do spend time together, it's the most epic time.

I was so tired and drained that I didn't want to eat anything. All I wanted to

15

do was curl up into my bed, and rest in it as though it was a tomb. There's a simple thing that no one tells you about death. That even though you're not the one dead, it feels like you are. I hated how much I missed Denise. I missed her smile, how she insisted on wearing "butterfly" by Bath and body works every single day, how her favorite thing to do was have me take photos of the outfit she had just sewed. I collapsed into my bed, and hugged the biggest pillow I had. I was frozen. Denise was gone, and I could feel myself falling away too. At that moment, I wanted Mark. To feel like I still had something. Everything in my life was telling me no; but for once I just wanted to say yes.

Chapter 4: Portraits

It was simple, until it wasn't.

I was walking down my staircase when I saw something on my porch. There was a small box and a blue rose. I didn't understand it. I hadn't ordered anything. I took it to my room and opened the little box. On top there was a note.

"I love how beautiful you knew Denise to be. I am so proud of you. Don't ever forget who you are. You've left a mark on me sweetheart"

Immediately I began crying again. Under the note, there was a necklace with an angel wing, music note, and a butterfly in it. I held it to my chest and I just knew. It was Mark.

After that day, things were different. Seeing that necklace really made me come to terms with how I felt about Mark. I wasn't sure, but it almost felt like Denise was egging me on. "You know you like him" she would've said, all giggly. The truth was, that even though I was not one of those girls, somehow I had fallen in love with him.

You know how I said that Wilhemina's is weird? Well, I meant how strict it was. There was always some rule to be followed, Like no phones in academic spaces, no speaking in classrooms unless a teacher says a certain phrase, you had to have as few absences as possible, the list goes on. I walked into class on April 28th. I had my favorite dress on, It was a little yellow mini with sunflowers and butterflies all over it. I sat in my usual seat in the back, and my teacher pulled down a projector screen. This was

shocking, only because at Wilhemina's the teachers tended to use as little

technology as they possibly could use. Someone turned out the lights and

the video started playing. There were the most beautiful art pieces I had

ever seen on that video. There was a sunflower, a drawing with a butterfly,

and a human heart. Weirdly there was a canvas with a simple dot on it. It

confused me, it was almost like there was a little mark on the... wait a

minute; and then a portrait came up. I couldn't believe my darned eyes.

That portrait was of me, with a butterfly in my afro, and a camera in my

hand.

The next picture was a picture of a corsage on the hand, and then Mark

came out from behind the screen with a bouquet of flowers. He looked me

directly in my eyes and asked me a question that I never in a million years

thought I would be asked. "Kemina-Marcheline, would you do me the

honors of allowing me to take you to prom?" I smiled and chuckled

"Mark... yes!"

The classroom at Wilhemina's goes absolutely crazy. Kids seemed so happy.

Girls that had never spoken to me before during my entire 12 years at that

school spoke to me after. It was something.

Mark and I began to realize ourselves after that. I found myself missing him

19

when he was gone, and loving every minute that he was with me. My favorite thing was him coming over to my house to watch a disney movie with me on Friday nights.

Mark always knocks a Rhythm on the door when he comes over. I had just put some popcorn on the stove when he came this Friday night. I ran to the door and opened it.

"Kemina-Marchelineeeeee" he exclaimed as he stretched out my name while walking in.

I chucked and gave him a hug

"You know what I'm thinking?" Mark said suspiciously

"What's that?" I asked, somewhat concerned

"That brownies sound delicious right about now"

I threw my head back in laughter, and grabbed the brownie pack out of his hand. We pulled out bowls and eggs and flour to start making the brownies. I turned to grab the vegetable oil from the cabinet and I felt something on my cheek.

"Mark! What the heck?!" I half-screamed, half-laughed. I quickly grabbed the powdered sugar and blew him a "kiss." This kiss was lethal though, I blew my hand, and the powder flew all over his face, turning him into a ghost.

I put the bag on the counter and ran for my life. Mark is much faster than me though, he took about 2 steps and countered my 5. He tackled me onto the couch and pinned me there. I felt bad for my mother, there was flour and powdered sugar all over my couch but I couldn't stop laughing.

It was all simple, until it wasn't.

Chapter 5: Colors

Mark and I laughed for a long time, neither of us moving. We didn't need to. After some time of simply staring into each other's eyes, Mark let me go.

"Unhand me, soldier" I laughed, rolling my eyes at him.

I went to my room to get a rag to clean up the couch.

When I got there I couldn't move, because I was so deep in thought. There was no way that I had fallen this hard for someone, for the only one friend that I've had since Denise. As I walked down the stairs with the towel and began to clean the couch my head filled with thoughts of her. Suddenly I felt nothing but sadness, and I broke down into tears. I felt bad, because Mark probably had no idea why I had just broken down, he just knew that I had.

"Kemina-Marcheline" he began, before he decided to just hold me tightly.

I woke up at 6:00 am. I don't remember going to bed, Mark must've brought me up after my break down. Leave it to me to take a wonderful date and ruin it. My eyes feel puffy and swollen, and my hands clammy. I wanted to do nothing but lay in my bed for the next 2 weeks. After a few minutes, I forced myself to arise when I noticed the blue roses in a jar on my dresser. I felt tears come to my eyes once more as I began to sob. The pain was almost unbearable. My phone rang for the third time in a row; it was Mark.

"Kemina-Marcheline" he almost shouted in the phone

"Mark, not now." I said, half tearfully, and half angrily.

"Please Kemina, I want to help you, I want you to let me in! I want to know

how you're feeling, I-" Mark's voice desperately stated.

"MARK." I almost yelled into the phone.

"I don't know how to let you in, I don't know if I want to let you in. For all

I know, you're just like everyone else at that school. You have NO idea what

I feel. You probably couldn't understand if you tried. Just leave me alone!"

The phone was silent for some time. It was a deafening silence. Almost like

a bomb had exploded, and there were just ashes falling everywhere.

Mark finally broke the silence.

"You should try me, Kemina-Marcheline. Just try me."

The call was disconnected.

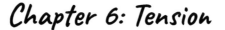

Chapter 6: Tension

It was simple, until it wasn't.

We established that Wilhemina's is hell, but without Mark, it was a hell that felt almost unbearable. For the first two days, we just walked past each other in the hall. He would look at me with the saddest eyes I've ever seen in him, but would continue walking. I wanted nothing more than to talk to him. To tell him that I didn't mean what I said, and that I was just grieving; but I felt the way I did as a child; speechless.

I was in chemistry once again, on the third day of the aftermath. We were learning about electron configuration, but I wasn't even paying attention. My mind stayed on Denise and Mark. How to fix the situation, How to honor her.

"Kemina, what's the electron configuration of Argon?"

Crap. Of course she would call on me for that.

"I-" I stuttered.

"Not so smart now are you?"

A voice called from the back of the room. Immediately I heard laughter and lots of voices giggling. I felt my tongue get stuck in my mouth and that I was unable to speak. My face got hot, and if I were any lighter, my skin would be as red as an apple. I grabbed my laptops and my bag and ran outside and left.

"Kemina-Marcheline!"

I jumped out of my bed, hearing my mother that angry scared me. I could hear her walking up the stairs and I attempted to come up with an excuse as to why I was at home, but stopped. I loved my mother, so hopefully when I tell her what happened she won't be as upset. Once the door opened, I knew what was up.

"Kemina-Marcheline you've got all of 3 seconds to start telling me why I received a call that you WALKED out of class today."

I could tell she was wanting the truth, not that I wouldn't have told her the truth, but it really matters right now.

"Mom, I couldn't. Kids started laughing at me while I was tongue tied, and-" Tears welled into my eyes once more;

"I just really miss Denise, and now there's so much tension with Mark, I just don't even know what to do! I just feel so alone, and I don't know what to do anymore."

My mother walked into my room, and sat down on the bed next to me. I felt bad, because all that I said probably sounded like an excuse, but it was really hurting me.

27

"Kemina-" She paused, and I saw the tears in her eyes too.

"Forgive me for yelling. You teenagers are going through alot in this chapter of your life. You're expected to figure out what college to attend, which can determine a lot of your life, while also having to learn chemistry. And you…" her voice trailed off.

She wiped a tear from her eye. I couldn't remember the last time I saw her cry.

"Honey, you've been through the unimaginable. You lost your best friend. Sometimes I think that you've healed from that, but I realized today that you will never truly heal from a loss like that. The pain may just become more tolerable."

"Mom, I loved her. I just don't understand why this happened to her. Why did she have to be the one?"

I sobbed.

"Bad things happen to good people. I couldn't tell you why, I don't know sweetheart. All I know is that you have to keep going." My mother lovingly said.

"I promise you, Denise, as hard-headed and spunky as she was; she wouldn't want you to spend your days crying about her. She would want you to take every photograph, sing every song, and do everything that makes

28

you happy. Do it for her, Kemina."

"And as for Mark, I've seen that boy. I trust him. And I don't think y'all's story is over just yet. Try and talk to him, I'm sure something will give. You have more than you think."

With that, she got up and walked back out of the door.

She doubled back

"Oh, you're grounded, by the way." She said with a wink.

I smiled, I wouldn't have had it any other way.

Chapter 7: Healing

It was simple, until it wasn't.

After talking to my mom, I realized that she was right. I needed to
continue on for Denise. I couldn't let myself rot in my bed on her account.

It was early Saturday morning, when I decided to go for a swim. I needed
the exercise, and I had found one of my father's old camera manuals. Turns
out, my camera is waterproof! There was a little pond that Denise and I
used to play in when we were little. There was this big set of rocks, from
where we stacked one every single month. I could tell that morning was
different, because I was actively thinking about Denise, and yet I felt hope,
and joy.

As I walked down the path, I felt overjoyed by the sight of the sunrise. It
was beautiful; the sky was purple, blue and pink. It was honestly a relief, I
felt like I could fly. As I got closer to the pond, I began to feel the ground
get soft beneath me, and I smiled. It was the mud! All of the memories of
Denise and I playing in this mud and getting dirty flooded my mind, and
suddenly I was so thankful for it. My camera continued clicking away.

Once I found the rock statue, I was in awe. Denise and I placed a stone
there every month. I got onto the ground and I took a picture. The rocks
made me smile, because I was reminded of the poems that she used to

write. Denise used to only read her poems in this spot, for the sole reason that it is her "firm foundation." I never really knew what that meant, but her poems were beautiful. I layed back and felt the grass. It was quiet, besides the sounds of the water and the dragonflies. I was at peace. I almost couldn't believe it! Laying in that grass made me think about my life. I can remember getting up, and taking a look at the water. It was cool and crisp. Looking into the water, I began to see something I had never seen before. For the first time, I looked into the water, and knew what I was looking at. When I saw my face in the water; I saw a beautiful girl. A girl that was smart. A girl who has been through the unimaginable, yet is able to smile. A girl who is talented in her work of photography and her music. The most beautiful part was that as I washed my hands in this pond, I felt cleaned. Cleaned of all stress, and pain in my body. I could feel Denise. It was like she was wrapping me in a hug. This trip brought me to the conclusion that no matter what, I wanted to pursue photography. I wanted to continue it for the rest of my life.

While I was there, I realized something that I had never realized before. I wasn't one of those girls, but I had fallen in love with Mark. That's why it hurt so bad to be away from him. I needed to go find him, and tell him how sorry I was. He deserved to know the truth if nothing else.

32

It was simple, until it wasn't.

Satisfied with my visit to the pond, I took off my muddy shoes and began to trek home. With my newfound confidence, I could have taken on the world. I had finally found myself.

Chapter 8: Reset

I got inside and immediately got a shower. I went and found my sunflower dress, and my white Converse. I had never gotten ready that quickly, but desperate situations call for desperate measures.

I ran downstairs and my mother saw me. She must have known what I was doing because she just nodded her head and allowed me to walk out the door. I drove to Mark's house. The whole way there, I was shaking like a jumping bean, trying to figure out what to say. When I turned to come down his street, I saw him putting a suitcase in the back of his truck. He stopped immediately, dropping his suitcase when he saw me.

"Kemina-" He stammered.

"Mark, I'm so sorry. About everything. It wasn't fair for me to say that, I was just hurting so-" I tried to explain.

I didn't even get to finish my explanation when Mark cut me off.

"Kemina, it's all good." Mark said, dryly.

"You should go, Kemina-Marcheline."

I couldn't believe what I heard. As he turned his back to put the suitcase and another bag into his truck, I stood there almost lost in time. Was it too late? Had I pushed him too far away? I can't lose him... No way. Not without a fight.

"No." I only said one, miniscule word yet it was more powerful than every yes I had ever stated.

He turned around, Slowly, Almost as though he did not believe what he heard.

"What did you say?"

He asked, almost softly.

"I said no, Mark. You came and you sat beside me in the hallway, not caring if someone laughed at you; you gave me a reason to want to come to school everyday, you asked me to prom in front of the whole class; with no shame. I'm so sorry, but to say that I'm not totally and utterly in love with you, would be for me to tell the biggest lie in the world. I will not go."

"What did you say?" He asked as he stepped towards me.

"Mark-" my voice trailed off.

And there it was. You know how every girl raves about having her first kiss? They almost act like it's what enters you into womanhood. Dramatic much? Mark grabbed my waist and pulled me into a kiss, bridal style and all. I had never kissed or kissed anyone, yet my lips seemed to know exactly what to do. I felt protected, safe. Then again- it was Mark. He's just like that. After what felt like an eternity and 5 seconds at the same time; he stopped. He still had those beautiful watercolor eyes that I could stare into forever.

"What is this suitcase for?" I asked, shifting an eyebrow

Mark chuckled a little bit.

"I was feeling some kinda way about us. I couldn't stand it. Not having you. I was going somewhere to clear my mind."

Typical Mark. A drive was always the plan A if something went wrong.

"Where are you driving to, Trucker?" I asked in a 1950's dialect. I earned a grin from Mark.

"How about New York?" He said.

New York? I think he's actually lost his mind.

"Are you being serious?" I could not wrap my mind around him actually wanting to drive to New York. But then again, he is Mark. This man leaves a mark on the world, and to do that, I guess you've got to go everywhere, right?

"100%, Kemina-Marcheline. 100%.

I want to drive through as many states as I possibly can. You know how you thought I wouldn't understand what you were feeling? Well, I do. All too much."

That broke my heart. I had a feeling he knew exactly how I was feeling, and that hurt me. I couldn't have wished that kind of pain on my worst enemy.

Suddenly, he grabbed my hand. I could tell by the way he was holding it, that he was feeling something. That my Mark was in pain. "Kemina-Marcheline, my father was in the military. He was a Captain. Last year, 3 soldiers were on my doorstep, holding a folded flag."

He paused. I could understand if he wanted to cry, I wanted to cry.

"My father was killed in battle. I know it's all respected to die in battle and what-not; but I just wanted my father."

How completely insensitive could I have been to say what I said to Mark. It was so ignorant. Mark began to wipe his face.

"Everything that I do, I do for him. Every painting and drawing is in honor of him. Every song I listen to, is in honor of him. It took me a long time to get to this point, but I choose to love everyone, because that's what my father did. He ultimately died for this country. That's a kind of love that I can only hope I can dish out."

"I love that so much Mark. I'm so sorry for your loss, but I'm so proud of what you've done with it. I hope to become like you. To be driven by the lost." I said, with complete sincerity.

It was silent for a little bit, but I didn't mind. I was so happy that the air felt open and optimistic again.

"With that all being said"

It was simple, until it wasn't.

He stated out of the blue. "I'm heading on this trip."

I decided to be bold.

"Then I'm going with you."

Mark was a little startled. "Kemina-Marcheline, what about school?"

"What about it?" I inquired. I walked around and got into the other side of his truck.

Mark had a laugh. A hearty laugh. "Kemina-Marcheline, I think you're nuts. Frankly, I don't know why you want to go."

I shook my head, "Mark, I need to do this. I need to."

I pulled my cell phone from the pocket on my dress, and opened a text to my mother.

"Hey, Mama. Please don't worry about me, I know you will be angry when I return home, but I promise that it's worth it. I just need you to trust me, Mama. I love you so much, and I can't wait to see you! I have to do this, for me."

I hit send, on the text and turned my phone off.

Mark looked over at me, with wide eyes. Silently asking permission to move his truck. I nodded my head yes, indulging his request.

I stared out the window, taking pictures of the trees passing by, when I caught him staring at me.

"Whattt?!" I whined. wanting to know the reason.

It was simple, until it wasn't.

"Oh nothing", he said with a grin.

"Just, I love you too, Kemina-Marcheline."

Chapter 9: Virginia

It was simple, until it wasn't.

The first stop of our adventure was in Virgina. It's ironic because I always thought the phrase "Virginia is for Lovers" was stupid. Mark and I got out of the car at Sunoco Gas Station in Amelia Court House, Virginia.

"You can get whatever you want, on me." Mark said while closing the door.

"Mark-" I began to protest

"Hush. I insist." He said, as he took my hand in his.

This was an interesting day. Virginia was an interesting place. Mark and I got some Jarritoes and went to sit on the back of his tailgate. I won't lie, being away from home was something that I didn't really have experience with, I mean; traveling wasn't something my family did. Mark and I sat on that truck observing the people of Virginia.

"Wait" I said, jumping off the truck bed. I reached into the car to grab my camera. It was the only thing I had brought besides a small toiletry bag.

Mark was chuckling when I got back to the tailgate. I snapped a quick picture of him, before he could notice what I was doing. I started taking pictures of some of the interesting things that were happening in front of us. It was a crazy ordeal, even though we were missing school; It seemed that I was learning so much more by taking photos and observing than I ever did in Wilhemina's.

"Kemina-Marcheline, Look!" Mark said, pointing to my left.

There was an older couple. They looked to be in their 70's or 80's. They were slow-dancing in the middle of the parking lot, as happy as they could possibly be. When I saw them, I saw exactly what I wanted out of life. What Denise would have wanted for me. I snapped the photo, when the two began to get into their car. Just as the man was about to get into the driver's seat, he turned to Mark and I and shouted:

"70 years!"

Maybe Virginia is for lovers

Mark and I stopped around 7pm, once we made it to the beach. I won't lie, I never liked the beach as a kid. I loved the water, its saltiness and the animals that inhabited it, but I hated the feeling of sand. As I've gotten older, it has gotten better, I can now tolerate sand; but I typically don't unless I have to.

The sun was beaming on the beach. It almost felt as though it was beating directly on Mark and I. I figured that by 8:30 or 9, the sun would go down, and the heat would stop. I pulled out my camera, and started taking pictures of the starfish, stuck to the big boulders on the shore. I heard Mark chuckle behind me.

"What?" I asked, laughing a little bit, myself.

"Oh, nothing." He said quickly

"Tell me" I said, pleading.

"Just, It's so cute how you pull out your camera every time you see something beautiful. It's almost like you wan't to capture it so that you can stick it in your pocket and keep it for later."

You know, I never thought of it that way, but it's true. I definitely got it from Denise. We used to take photos of everything we saw, and then we would look back at them every night. It was our way of reclaiming time.

Mark and I took off our shoes and started walking towards the shore.

Interestingly, it was warm, but the water was cool. I began to line up, to try to get a shot of the water reflecting on the waves. Once I got it, Mark splashed water on me. He better be glad my camera is waterproof! I took off after him, kicking sand and water into the air. He ran all the way back to the truck, trying to find safety; but was unsuccessful. I took the camera off, placed it in the back of the truck and it was on.

I ran straight into the ocean after Mark, getting soaked. Of course, when I decided to come on this impromptu road trip, I didn't bring a swimsuit, however my dress would do just fine. I could feel the seawater getting into my hair and my skin. I could smell the ocean in the air surrounding us, and I felt alive. Eventually, I got tired; the water had drawn the heat from me. I sat down, and felt the sand find its way into every crevice of my skin. Mark came and sat down beside me. We didn't speak for almost an hour, but we watched the sun sink down into the horizon. The sunset was breathtaking, and it once again reminded me of all the beauty that fills the Earth, as we look around it. My favorite part of Virginia was how it was the first night that I didn't have a cellphone at all. My phone was turned off and in the glove box of Mark's truck. For once, I was able to experience all of that beauty, just my camera, Mark, and I. It was the most incredible experience I think I have ever had, even to this day. I have never been able to recreate the feeling that I had on that Virginia beach. Just the sand, water, sun and

Mark; yet I had fallen in love with life.

Yeah. Maybe Virginia is for Lovers.

It was simple, until it wasn't.

Chapter 10: Stargazing

It was simple, until it wasn't.

We dried off using some towels that we found in Mark's truck, and we found a small sandwich shop a few blocks down. We decided to save gas and walk to the shop. We ordered sandwiches, and fries to share, and then headed back to the truck. It was getting dark so Mark and I decided to weigh out our options for where to sleep.

"We could try to find a hotel." Mark suggested.

"Mark, it's like 8:30 pm. Most places are probably booked for the night. Besides, I think I like the beach." I noted slyly.

I earned a chuckle from Mark. "That is true, we should probably save what little money we have. Beach it is."

The two of us layed back in the bed of the truck and started to observe the sky; the stars were gorgeous and bright.

"Look, It's Orion" Mark said, pointing to my right.

"The O- what?" I asked, confused."

He laughed, outwardly this time. "Kemina-Marcheline; the Orion constellation. It was named after the Hunter, back in Greek Mythology. It's been around for a long time too."

"How do you know that the stars you're looking at are actually the Orion?"

I asked, very curiously now.

"The Orion holds two of the brightest stars in the Milky Way. So typically when you see those stars together, it's a good indicator that it's Orion. Plus, it feels like an Orion type night."

That made me laugh. It was one of the things that I enjoyed about Mark. No matter where we were, or who we were talking to, Mark always seemed to be fully himself. This meant that I always could tell how he was feeling, because he always let it be known. He's just a comforting soul to be around, and I consider myself to be very lucky.

"Next time I'm out on a road trip to California, I'll be sure to look for the Orion" I laughed.

"Who would you be with for a road trip all the way to California?" He asked, raising an eyebrow.

"Hm, I don't know, " I said flirtatiously.

"Probably someone who is smart, but also kind. Someone who's strong, but tender. Someone who loves art, and someone that has long hair…"

Mark laughed. "Kemina-Marcheline, you… are… crazy."

We both burst into laughter, and laid back into the truck bed.

"I haven't felt like this in a long time, Kemina-Marcheline. I think I've been really numb since my dad died. But then you came along." He said, affectionately.

We stared at the sky and were comforted by each other's presence.

"Mark, do you know where you want to go? For college?" I asked. I needed to figure it out for myself, acceptances were coming out soon.

"I think I want to go to the school of the arts. In Winston-Salem. I want to get better at classical art." He responded.

He's so cute. He always lights up when he talks about his future or art.

"I love that, Mark. I'm so proud of you, really. I can't wait to see all the wonderful things you will do. The Mark you're gonna leave on the world."

"The takeover has begun," he said in a dark voice.

We earned a bunch of laughs, and once again it became quiet. Just the two of us, admiring God's work. He pulled me closer, and before I knew it, we fell asleep.

Right under the stars.

It was simple, until it wasn't.

Chapter 11: Maryland

We left Virginia that morning, around 11am. Mark and I were groggily awake around 6, to see the sunrise, but we fell back asleep around 7. Having little sleep is new to me, honestly I like it. It makes everything around me that much more surreal.

We both reeked of sea-water, and we made a decision not to get into any more water for the trip unless it was a shower. Speaking of which, we needed showers. To say that we probably smelled was an understatement. As funny as it is, Mark is the only person I would trust myself to be smelly around. He just wouldn't judge me like that.

We reached Maryland about four hours later, and we decided to try and find a hotel for the night. We both were in desperate need of showers, and could use some hygiene. We were able to find one, and we put our stuff down in the room. Once we got our showers, we decided to go to the aquarium.

During this trip, I learned that I have a love for people. Even though I never was close with a lot of people, I loved observing their actions and decisions. It was just interesting.

In the Aquarium, I realized that I also loved fish. Mark and I spent 7 hours simply watching fish swim around. Of course, I pulled my camera out; and I turned off the flash. Click, click, click away I went. Taking

pictures was one of my favorite things to do, and seeing as I enjoy fish, it

turned out to be a pretty fun day. We decided to go to the shop, where they

even had a mermaid! I snapped away, and Mark and I stayed until the

aquarium closed.

On the way back to the hotel, we saw a group gathered in the street,

around a singer.

"Mark, let's go hear her" I asked, my parents could vouch for me, I

always loved street music. Being in Harlem during the cultural revolution

wouldn't have been a bad thing for me, because I just loved music so much.

Mark pulled the truck into a nearby lot and we got out. The singer was

beautiful; she had the longest and straightest blond hair that I had ever seen.

Her eyes were a beautiful green, almost reminding me of the seafoam at the

beach Mark and I went to in Virginia. As she strummed her guitar, and

sang, her voice was so smooth, it almost reminded me of butter.

"Why is it so hard for us to love one another, and care for eachother, and play like we're

brothers, and when will we look past the surface, finding out our true purpose, that would

be a world that I like."

It was simple, until it wasn't.

Mark held out his hand. At first I was unsure of what he was doing, and I attempted to give him a high-five! I earned a chuckle from him but he never removed his hand. I then placed the small flower I was holding in his hand; before he shook his head at me. I gave my hand to him, and with a kiss, he pulled me into a dance.

I laughed; "Mark, you know I can't dance, right?!"

He laughed back; "I can tell by the way you're stepping on my feet!!"

Slowly, I figured out how to do the old-timey waltz that they do in movies. I almost wanted to find a top hat for Mark. Dancing in the middle of Maryland, to a singer that we've never heard of quickly became my favorite memory. Mark and I danced for about an hour, before we decided to call it quits for the night.

"Mark, I'm hungry" I said, quickly; trying to pull off of the street. We had started a trend, and we saw lots of other couples dancing to the music. I was thankful too, it got the singer more tips!

"Wait!" I ran to the side and grabbed my camera from the side.

"Hey! Can I get a picture with you?!" I called out to the singer. She shook her head yes; and I grabbed Mark's hand, and we ran over to her. I held the camera up and pointed the lens towards the three of us. With a smile; I snapped the photo.

I later found out that her name was Molori, and she ended up releasing the song "A world that I like" the following night. As I went to sleep that night, I smiled, as I replayed the events of the day. One of the lyrics she sang really touched me.

""When we laugh, we find a deeper connection, and while we dance; I feel the resurrection of our true selves; we form a community, unity."

This made me think; the more laughs I experience, the more I think I find myself. That's why this trip has been so important. The only thing left is to get to New York; and I can't wait to see the "concrete jungle of dreams" that Alicia told me about.

It was simple, until it wasn't.

Chapter 12: New York

Mark and I decided that we wanted to spend 2 days in New York, because at that point we had been gone for 3 days, and we decided at most we would be gone for 5 days. We got up at 4am, in the wee hours of the morning, and began to drive. The drive was a little long; about 3.5 hours. We passed the time by finding random artists to listen to on the radio. After about an hour of this, Mark reached over and turned the radio off.

"Whyyy" I whined.

"Because" he started, chuckling at my sore reaction. "I wanna hear one of your songs. I know you play guitar, and piano; and I know you can sing too.

I remember chuckling; the sun had just started to wake up and I could feel the small amount of heat peering through the window that would exist at 6 in the morning. I turned on a track and began to hum. This was new to me, I always wrote songs for other people, but never ones to sing for myself.

"I wrote this one, while we weren't talking, I felt so alone and upset; you know?" He nodded his head.

"This song is called Drifting."

"Are we drifting? Because I'm missing you. I don't wanna shift dynamics, cause, I know, that I will panic, when I'm missing you…"

When I finished singing the song, Mark didn't say anything for a minute. "That was… that was beautiful, Kemina-Marcheline. I've never heard anything like it. We're gonna have to find you a producer in New York!'

I laughed. "I'm excited for New York! I'm wondering if it's anything like the movies, or how the songs make it seem."

"I don't know, Kemina-Marcheline. I've never been, but honestly I'm imagining it to be absolutely wonderful; like a dream come true.

We arrived in New York about an hour and a half later; it was about 7:30 am. As we pulled into one of the few places to park, Mark asked me "Where to?" I shook my head, "I'm not sure, I've never been to New York.."

He chuckled. "Are you hungry? I heard New York has some bomb bagels."

We ended up stopping at a place called "Happy's" and I kid you not, they had at least 30 different bagels. Mark and I settled on sharing a "pizza' bagel and I will be the first one to say; it was delicious. We had bagel shops in North Carolina; but none were even on the same level as this one.

"Kemina-Marcheline" Mark said, chewing softly.

"This just.. might be the best thing, I've ever tasted"

I shook my head. "Better than my brownies?"

He laughed heartily; "If I say yes, how long do I have to finish this piece before you run me out of here?"

I raised an eyebrow; "2 seconds."

We spent the first day of New York merely walking around; enjoying the city. The sun was beaming; yet it wasn't hot, the street music was beautiful and the feeling of Mark's hand in mine left me feeling as though the world was mine. I enjoyed an art gallery that Mark and I saw. It had the most beautiful works; sculptures, paintings, and a mural. This was Mark's jam. I could see how happy being in there made him. I remember wondering how he came to find that he loved art.

"Mark?" I started, tugging his sleeve down.

"Yes, Kemina-Marcheline?"

I giggled, it still made me internally blush when he called my real name.

"How did you come to love art?"

He didn't reply for a minute, he was thinking about something.

"Honestly, I started drawing once my father was deployed. We would always send letters to him, and I started sending drawings. Sometimes we would get letters back from his mates, who also loved my drawings; they said it brought light to their worlds. They were the first to call me Mark." He laughed a little bit. I could tell that talking about his dad made him happy.

"And it just kind of started like that. I don't know when I got "good" at it, or anything; but all I know is that I want to draw and create for the rest of my life. I've always told myself that I'm going to be a doctor, but who am I kidding? I can live without medicine, but I can't live without art."

When Mark said that, it hit me really hard. For once, it made me understand what it meant to choose a life in which I would be truly happy. I thought that this trip would help me figure out who I am, but I didn't realize that it would help me determine what I wanted to do. In that moment I realized that the same way Mark needs art in his life so desperately, I needed photography in mine. I need to be a photographer. I have to be a photographer.

"Hey Mark?" I asked once more.

He looked over at me, raising an eyebrow softly.

"I have a request, before we leave? I need to tour a place."

He chuckled, "yes. But tomorrow. Tonight we have something special."

I was confused, I thought this art museum was our special thing.

I begged and pleaded but I could not get an answer out of him. All he said

was to wear my sunflower dress, and to meet him in our hotel lobby. I

remember quickly showering, and picking out my afro. It seemed to have

gotten longer and thicker since I left. I applied a little bit of mascara and

lipgloss, before grabbing my jean jacket and heading down to the lobby.

There he was. Mark was at the bottom of the stairs, holding the most

beautiful red roses. He had on all black, and he had pulled his hair back.

"You clean up real nice, sir." I teased, as I gave him a hug.

We ended up going to an Italian restaurant, and at about 6:50, Mark pulled

out a black piece of fabric, and instructed me to blindfold myself. At this

point, I knew something was going on, but I had no idea what it could've

been. Something about being blindfolded at night in New York scared me,

but something about having Mark by my side took away all my fears.

We walked for a little bit, maybe 10 minutes, before I was to sit in a

seat. Mark counted down from 10 for me to remove the blindfold, and when I removed it, we were still in a dark area. Suddenly lights turned on, and I heard the call of Rafiki. Immediately I looked at Mark, shocked.

"Is this-?" I started, barely able to speak

"Yes. Welcome to Broadway, Kemina-Marcheline."

The Lion King had been one of the few movies I watched as a child that stuck with me. I had always loved the plot of it, and the music was brilliant. Even with that being said, the broadway version exceeded every expectation I had, and then some. The costumes, the acting, the music; if this was the true New York experience, I wouldn't mind living here.

When the show ended, I still was in disbelief. Here I was, miles upon miles away from home, I hadn't touched my phone in 4 days and I had just seen my first Broadway show. It was almost like a dream. As Mark and I walked to our hotel, there was one thing in particular that happened. I don't know why, nor how, but a blue butterfly sat on my forehead. I looked up, noticing its beautiful wings, and yet it stayed on my forehead. Mark gently pulled the camera from my hands and took a picture of the beautiful scene. After a minute or so, the butterfly gracefully lifted itself into the air, and fluttered away.

That was how I knew that Denise would never truly leave us.

The next morning Mark and I packed everything up, and loaded up his truck for the last time. This would be the end of our extravagant, unplanned trip across the world. I loved New York, but I missed my mother. I was so glad to finally be going home. As I got situated, Mark began to drive. We only drove 20 minutes, before Mark started to slow down and stop.

"Mark, we just started moving, you have to pee already?" I joked.

I earned an eye roll and laugh from Mark.

"No, silly. We have one more stop we need to make before we go home."

When I got out of the car, I realized where we were. We were at the Eugene Lang College of Liberal Arts. I knew that if I wanted to become a photographer, this was one of the best places to go. As I stood there, I realized that perhaps this was it. This was right where I was supposed to be.

This is it. This is where I realized how hard of a decision I would be making. My life was simple. My friends, my story, even my school. All of it was simple. My life had been totally simple until it wasn't. As I got back in the car, thinking of the school; I suddenly couldn't wait to get home, to see

It was simple, until it wasn't.

my mother. I needed her advice. I needed her.

It was simple, until it wasn't.

Chapter 13: Home, sweet, Home.

It was simple, until it wasn't.

On the way in, I grabbed flowers for my mother. I knew that it wouldn't be nearly enough to console her for what I did, but maybe it would soften the blow, just a little bit.

Mark dropped me off in my driveway before I slowly walked into my house. I couldn't even come up with a way to explain our trip to my mother, and how much it meant to me. I walked into the kitchen, and there my mother was; her head in her hands. I placed the flower in the empty vase on the kitchen table, before walking and holding her hands.

Immediately when she saw me, I felt tears form in my eyes, and I saw them in hers. She didn't even say anything, before she pulled me into an embrace. It felt good to be home. We sat down on the couch, before she asked me a simple question.

"Honey, did you learn anything?"

Without a shout-of a doubt, the answer was yes.

I told her the whole story, Virginia, Maryland, New York. She clung to every word I said. When I explained that both Mark and I were healing, she really understood.

"Baby, I'm so glad that you're home. But I'm even more glad that you finally learned how to manage your grief. I'm so proud of you, Kemina-Marcheline."

Finally, I understood. For a long time, I wondered why my mother named me Kemina-Marcheline. Why did she believe me to be a strong warrior from the moment I took a breath on this earth? Suddenly I understood. I had been through something that should have broken me, something that should have shut me down, something that hurt me. Yet after a bit of time, I learned to look it in the eye. I learned that my grief cannot control me, and that love is the answer. I learned how to live in those 5 days with Mark.

I finally found Kemina-Marcheline.

It was simple, until it wasn't.

Chapter 14: Choices

It was simple, until it wasn't.

Returning to school and normal life was, to say the least, interesting. Of course people at school were talking, and spreading the craziest rumors imaginable. Some even made jokes that I had been arrested. Although I knew about what they were saying, it became the least of my concerns.

College admissions were coming out that week and Mark and I were getting ready for our senior prom. We worked out most of the details, except I had no dress, and prom was in 2 days. I was unsure of what to do, as I had never actually gone to a formal dance, and of course I did not have a dress. After school, I decided to walk downtown and look at some of the stores, just in case there was a dress for me. I hesitate to call myself picky, but I am very peculiar about what I wear, and dresses usually don't make the cut. As I walked downtown, another blue butterfly sat on my forehead. I know, it sounds crazy and unbelievable, but I promise it happened. It was only weird that it occurred twice. When I looked up, I saw a beautiful blue and purple sky. After a minute, the butterfly flew off into the distance. Even though I was walking alone, I could feel the wind wrapping me in a hug. I looked up at the sky, thankful for the wonderful environment surrounding me.

When I turned the corner, there was a little thrift shop. It was small, and not many people went inside. I decided I would try something new, even though I didn't believe there would be anything worthwhile in the shop. When I walked through the door, I was proven incorrect. Hanging up on the display was the most beautiful blue dress. It was tar-heel blue and had little silver decals on it. I pulled it down, and went to try it on. Miraculously, the dress fit; and at that moment, I realized that the butterfly had led me to my prom dress. If that isn't the weirdest thing I've ever experienced, I don't know what is.

I bought the dress, and began to head home for the night. When I got into the house, I heard my computer beep. I was confused, as it only beeps for emails. When I opened the latest email, it read:

"Congratulations! We are so excited to offer you admission into the Eugene Lang College of Liberal Arts, under the major of Film and Photography."

I couldn't believe it! I had actually been accepted to my dream school; I had no choice but to go. I can't imagine my life without photography, it's such a big part of me that without it, I don't know who I am. I ended up running the rest of the way home to show my mother.

"Mom!" I screamed, running through the door.

"What?" I'm sure I scared her, but I couldn't contain my excitement.

She ran down the stairs, and I just handed her my phone. It took her a minute before she started jumping and screaming with me.

"Kemina-Marcheline, this is wonderful! I'm so incredibly proud of you."

This was such an important moment for me. My future suddenly didn't seem so far away. I finally felt like I had control of my future, that it was going to be exactly what I made it to be. I was excited.

The end of senior year seemed to fly by after my acceptance. Mark got accepted into UNCSA for visual arts. We decided to do the best we could, but we understood that being together long distance would be difficult. We shifted our priorities to making the most of the time that had left.

Remember that client that my mother had? Well I did the photoshoot for her, and I am proud to say I did well. I landed an internship with the modeling agency that she was a part of, the second I sent her photos to her. This was exciting for me, as portrait photography was totally out of my comfort zone. I'm proud to say that I've done a lot of things to get myself out of my comfort zone in the past few months.

The day of prom was crazy. No one made me aware that girls would leave half-way through the day to get their hair and nails all prom-ready. I was still so swooned by the blue dress that the butterfly had led me to. Mark was planning to be in my foyer at 6:30 on the dot. As I retouched my hair, and applied some mascara, I felt myself smile.

Denise and I always dreamed of prom day. Every Disney movie that depicted a prom made our little expectations even higher. As I strapped my silver heels, I could feel how proud she would be of me. I could feel how proud I was of myself. As I walked down the stairs, I saw Mark's facial expression. One thing about him is that he will always make me feel like I'm the prettiest girl in the room. At that moment, it didn't matter what anyone else thought about me. At that moment, I knew I was beautiful without anyone having told me.

Prom was pretty cool. I mean, the DJ was terrible, but seeing as it's a school-sponsored event, I don't know what I expected. Mark's food choices made up for it though. He managed to get a pizza bagel sent all the way down from New York to us. It was a brilliant way to remind us of the wonderful times we had.

I had never slow-danced before either, but Mark insisted. I only obliged because it was Mark and I's last prom. We danced in a small box, going forwards, backwards, side to side. Mark was a good sport about it too, even though I stepped on his toes for most of the dance. Mark and I finished off prom with a little picnic in the park. He had set it up earlier in the day, and we were surrounded by candlelight. I was so glad that my first and only school dance went as well as it did. Of course, it being with Mark only sweetened the deal.

Once prom hit, I realized that the days were winding down. Fast. Suddenly, I found myself buying a white dress for graduation. It brought me great joy to be graduating from Wilhemina's. Although I had a hard and rocky road with Wilehemina's, it still was a massive part of my life. For it to no longer be a part of my life is weird. Like, I can't imagine my life any other way. This is a time for new beginnings. All of my choices up to this point of my life have paved the road I have, and all the choices that I will make will pave my path that's left to come.

It was simple, until it wasn't.

Chapter 15: The end, yet the beginning

It was simple, until it wasn't.

On May 26th, I received my high school diploma. I can still remember them calling my name, because I felt immense joy in that moment. I had on a white dress with black converses, and of course Mark was never far behind. Mark and I decided to savor the final summer. He was headed to the University of North Carolina School of the Arts in the fall, while I was headed to the Eugene Lang College of Liberal Arts. Long names, to say that one is in North Carolina, while the other is in New York. I spent my final summer taking pictures! In fact, I opened my own photography business, and I actually had gotten myself to the point of having steady clients. Of course, I planned to continue the business in New York.

One thing that people never warn of is the heartbreak that comes with graduation. I realized that it would be almost impossible to see Mark, and it took a toll on our relationship. Not in a negative way, but it made us think about our future. We decided it was better to break up prior to my moving to New York. I figured that if we were truly meant to be, we would find our way back to one another.

My senior year was something. During it, a lot of incredible things happened. I learned how to cope with the loss of Denise, but I also learned how to love Mark. I had finally found my passion, yet I also found my

career. I'm so proud of this year. I grew so much as an artist and as a

person. When I walked the stage, it was a monumental moment, not just

because I was graduating highschool but because I'm now on to begin the

rest of my life. Mark came with my Mom to drop me off at school. Him and

I considered it our "last date" and we filled it with happy memories. We

went to see a show, art gallery, and of course, we found our famous pizza

bagels to nibble on the day before. At 9am, we dropped all of my baggage

off with the bagger, and as he took it to my dorms; I had to say my final

goodbyes.

"I love you." I said, fighting to hold back the tears as I hugged my mother.

She truly was my rock, and to know that she would be so far hurt a little bit.

"I'm always so proud of you, my Kemina," she said, sniffling as well.

"Make sure to send me a million photos, and whenever you start

photographing for big time companies-"

"Mom!" I laughed. She had high ideas, but then again, so did I.

I slowly walked over to Mark. It hurt my heart to be saying goodbye to him.

We had been through a lot this past year.

"Kemina-Marcheline" He started, immediately pulling me into a hug.

"I'm not going to say much, because words can't describe the love I have in my heart for you. Whenever you need an artist, you know who to call." He said quickly, I could tell he was trying to contain himself too.

I knew that part of my journey would have to end, for my new one to begin, but I am forever grateful for those who were a part of it. Mark and my mother got into the car, waved and just like that, they were gone.

As I stand here, at the door of the Eugene Lang College of Liberal Arts, my mind just races. I'm thinking so many thoughts, seeing so many things, hearing so many sounds, I can see a future here. Or do I. All I have ever wanted is to step somewhere where I feel accepted. To step into a circle where I can really say "I'm Home" (that isn't my room of course.) As I stare at that water-clear glass door, I can't help but think of all the memories, of all the days I've waited for this. I've also said that this was my dream, but now that it's here; I'm feeling shaky. I know, I know, no time to feel shaky when your destiny awaits you. It's like my whole life I've been pushing on the door that I'm staring into, but now that I'm finally here, I feel excitement, to see what my next journey is. Of course I want this.

As I walked to grab the handle of the door, I stopped. I had this sudden urge to look up at the sky, so I did. Interestingly enough, there was a

blue butterfly fluttering in the wind. It landed on my nose, and I knew.

That was my favorite part about this year, about all of the wonderful things

I had learned. Death, grief, love, passion, all of it is simple in its own accord.

It was all simple until someone came along to show me that there was more,

that my life is what I make it, not what happens to me.

It was all so simple, until it wasn't.

ABOUT THE AUTHOR

It was simple, until it wasn't.

Chelsea Victoria, is a creative artist from Greensboro, North Carolina. "It was simple until it wasn't" is her first published literary work as a new college student. When she isn't writing, she can be found writing music, practicing photography, or reading amazing books. She loves the outdoors and encouraging people. She simply encourages her readers to continue to go beyond their comfort zone, and to learn more about themselves. Chelsea Victoria wants to remind her readers to never stop dreaming, and chase every path that they may set foot on.

It was simple, until it wasn't.

A letter from Molori:

Hey, y'all!

My name is Molori and I was born and raised in Greensboro, North Carolina. Growing up, I was always interested in learning new things and exploring the world around me. As a child, I loved spending time outdoors, music, and reading books. After graduating from middle school, I attended a nearby performing arts high school where I majored in Recording Engineering. During my time in high school, I developed a deep passion for writing, performing, and producing. I spent countless hours writing songs, performing them, and eventually producing them. During my Sophomore year, I decided to pursue my dream of becoming an entrepreneur and owning my brand. I worked odd jobs to make ends meet while I wrote short stories, poems, and songs. I also found a passion for photography, just as my father had. Eventually, one of my poems was accepted for publication, and I knew I had found my calling. Over the years, I have continued to write and publish stories, songs, and photography both online and in print. I have dreams to work as a freelance songwriter, author, producer, and photographer, creating content for businesses and organizations. In addition to writing, I enjoy traveling, hiking, and spending time with my family and friends. Looking back on my life so far, I am grateful for the opportunities I have had and the people I have met. I am excited to see what the future holds and where my passions will take me next.

Don't you dare stop dreaming,

Molori xoxo